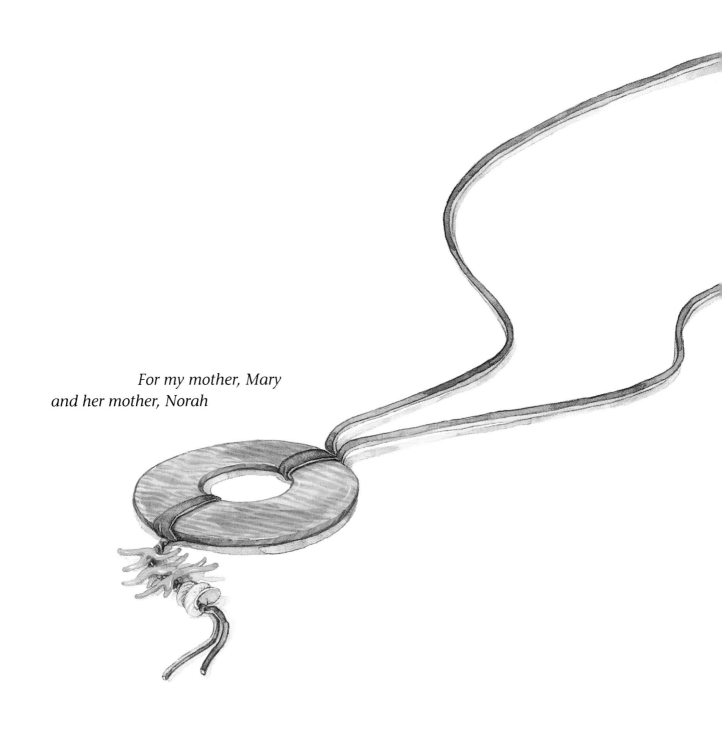

*For my mother, Mary
and her mother, Norah*

Sydor, Colleen, 1960 -
Smarty Pants
Text copyright © 1999 by Colleen Sydor
Illustrations copyright © 1999 by Suzane Langlois

Published by
Lobster Press Limited
1250 René-Lévesque Blvd. West, Suite 2200
Montréal, Québec H3B 4W8
Tel. (514) 989-3121 • Fax (514) 989-3168
www.lobsterpress.com

Edited by Jane Pavanel

Canadian Cataloguing in Publication Data

ISBN 1-894222-06-7

I. Langlois, Suzane   II. Title

PS8587.Y36S63 1999   jC813'.54   C99-900679-7
PZ7.S98276Sm 1999

Printed and bound in Canada

Smarty Pants

A Norah Book

Written by
Colleen Sydor

Illustrated by
Suzane Langlois

Lobster Press Limited

"Good day, Norah." "Good day, Norah."
That's the way my auntie and I always greet one another.
Auntie Norah is the woman I was named after. She's my mom's aunt,
which makes her my great-aunt. And she is. Great, that is. That's
why I always ask to stay with her when my mom is away on business.
"How long do we get this time?" asked Auntie, taking my suitcase.
"A week."
"Goody!" she said, rubbing her hands together.

"Did you bring the pretzels?"

I nodded. "Suitcase. Bottom left-hand corner. Did you get the cream soda?"

"Fridge," she answered. "Top left-hand shelf." Then she beamed. "So what are we waiting for? Let the games begin!"

Auntie Norah is the only adult I know who actually likes playing Snakes and Ladders. When she lands on a ladder, she's the happiest woman in the world. When she ends up on a snake, she needs cheering up.

"Hey Auntie," I'll say as she gloomily slides down the snake. "Why did the one-handed man cross the road?"

"Darned if I know, Love," she'll grumble.

"Why did the one-handed man cross the road?"

"To get to the second-hand store!"

At times like that Auntie Norah tries hard not to crack a smile. But she always ends up exploding, spit and giggles flying everywhere. Auntie hugs herself when she laughs. Sometimes I can even make her snort. On such occasions she reaches for anything in sight – the TV guide, an old pretzel bag, her hankie – and says, "Here, autograph this. One day you're going to be famous." I like to think she's right.

I love it when Auntie laughs at my jokes. Not everyone thinks they're funny. In fact, some people think I'm a little unusual.

"So who wants to be usual?" That's what Auntie Norah always says, and I'm inclined to agree with her. That's probably why Auntie Norah and I get along so well. She's a little unusual herself.

"Roll the dice, Auntie. Roll the dice!" I'll say impatiently when it's her turn. But she won't. First she'll cup the dice tenderly in her hands and whisper to it. The closer she is to winning, the longer she'll whisper. Then she'll cross her toes, blow on the dice three times and let it fly!

Auntie is like that. She's superstitious. I'm not. At night when we go for a walk I tell her, "Live dangerously Auntie. Step on a crack or two." But she won't. Never ever. That's just the way she is.

At the end of every day Auntie blows on the good luck medallion she wears around her neck and shines it with her hankie. "It's been a lucky day," she'll say. "Not everyone's as lucky as you and me, Norah." Then just before bed she'll say, "Now remember, always get into bed on the right-hand side, never the left, and before folding your clothes give them three hard shakes."

Usually I go along with Auntie's strange superstitions and rituals, but one night I felt stubborn.

"Auntie Norah," I said. "I'll get into bed on the right-hand side if it makes you feel better, but I'm not going to give my clothes three hard shakes. It's just too silly. In fact, I'm going to leave them in a pile right here on the floor."

Auntie went pale. She thought for a moment, then said, "I suppose a girl's gotta' do what a girl's gotta' do, but heaven help you tomorrow."

"Why?" I asked. "What could possibly happen if I don't give my clothes three hard shakes?"

"Something eye-popping, heart-stopping, holy-moly horrible," she said, "that's what."

"Auntie, you don't really believe that, do you?"

Auntie didn't answer. I heard her in the next room giving her clothes three extra-hard shakes.

"Good night, Norah," I called.

"Good night, Norah," she called back.

The next morning I stepped straight into my wrinkled clothes. Auntie Norah insisted I wear her good luck medallion to school, just in case. She also made me throw salt over my left shoulder on the way out the door.

I have to admit I spent most of that day feeling slightly nervous, even though I'm not superstitious. I half-expected something holy-moly horrible to happen. And it just about did. In math class I heard a bang and thought I was a goner. I nearly fell off my chair. It turned out it was only Barbara-Jane Anderson popping her paper lunch bag in my ear.

At recess I knew for sure it was all over when I saw Bully-face Barton thundering toward me. I got down on my hands and knees and begged for mercy. But he shot right past me. It turned out he was only going after a Frisbee.

As the day wore on I had to laugh at myself for being so foolish. At three o'clock Mrs. Ogorski said, "Class, it's time for Show and Share. Barbara-Jane and Norah, I believe it's your turn."

Barbara-Jane went first. She got out a strange-looking contraption and made Freddy Minetti model it so she wouldn't ruin her hair.

"This," she said grandly, "is a brolly hat. When it's raining, why carry a clumsy umbrella when you can leave your hands free for more important things?"

At that particular moment her hands were fluffing her thick brown curls. I rolled my eyeballs.

When it was my turn I took off Auntie Norah's good luck medallion, intending to pass it around. But before I could say a word, Barbara-Jane had her hand up.

"Norah," she said, "what is that?"

She was pointing at my foot. Something pink was poking out the bottom of my jeans. I held it up to have a better look. I shouldn't have done that. It was yesterday's undies. How eye-popping, heart-stopping, holy-moly horrible!

When I got home from school that day Auntie Norah was waiting anxiously at the door.

"Thank goodness you're still in one piece," she said. "I was worried sick." She checked me over from head to toe. "Did anything terrible happen?"

"Nope," I said. "Something wonderful happened. But I did find out why you should always give your clothes three hard shakes."

"Why?" asked Auntie Norah.

"So that yesterday's undies don't fall out during Show and Share."

"No!" said Auntie Norah. "How horrible. What did you do?"

"I put them on my head."

Auntie's jaw dropped. "You did what?!"

"I said to the class, 'This is a smarty-pants hat. On cold days, why suffer with hat hair when you can keep your ears warm and your pigtails happy at the same time?'"

Auntie Norah blasted a laugh and hugged herself extra-tight.

"What happened then?" she snorted.

"They laughed so hard I decided to tell them the joke about the one-handed man. That went over so well I told them every last one of my jokes. Auntie, I was a hit!"

"Of course you were," said Auntie Norah, giving me a squeeze and pressing her cheek against mine. She made me autograph my undies for her right then and there. She said she's going to have them framed so she can show them to all her friends when I'm famous. I'm looking forward to that.

These days when we go for a walk at night, Auntie Norah steps on a crack every now and then just to live dangerously. As for me, I never go to bed without giving my clothes three hard shakes.